# BARBARA D. BOOTH / JIM LAMARCHE
# MANDY

## LOTHROP, LEE & SHEPARD BOOKS    NEW YORK

This book is dedicated to Nana B and to the girls of Troop 304 at WSD, especially Sara    —BDB

To my sons, Mario, Jean-Paul, and Dominic    —JLM

Text copyright © 1991 by Barbara D. Booth    Illustrations copyright © 1991 by Jim LaMarche

Library of Congress Cataloging in Publication Data    Booth, Barbara D. Mandy / Barbara D. Booth ; illustrated by Jim LaMarche.    p.    cm.    Summary: Hearing-impaired Mandy risks going out into the scary night, during an impending storm, to look for her beloved grandmother's lost pin.    ISBN 0-688-10338-3.—ISBN 0-688-10339-1 (lib. bdg.)    [1. Hearing disorders—Fiction.    2. Physically handicapped—Fiction.    3. Grandmothers—Fiction.]    I. LaMarche, Jim, ill.    II. Title.    PZ7. B6463Man    1991    [E]—dc20    90-19989    CIP    AC

GRANDMA WAS STANDING NEAR THE SINK, tapping her fingers on the counter and moving her lips as she stared out the window. She's singing, thought Mandy, and she looked to see if the radio light was on. Grandma had told her that music and talk came out of the little black box on the windowsill, but Mandy's hearing aid couldn't be turned high enough to let her hear the sound. She had never heard anyone talk or sing, and she wondered about voices.

Once, Grandma had said that her mother's voice sounded sweet and soft. Mandy had put a half-eaten marshmallow to her ear, hoping to feel the sweet softness of her mother's voice, but she'd only ended up with a sticky ear.

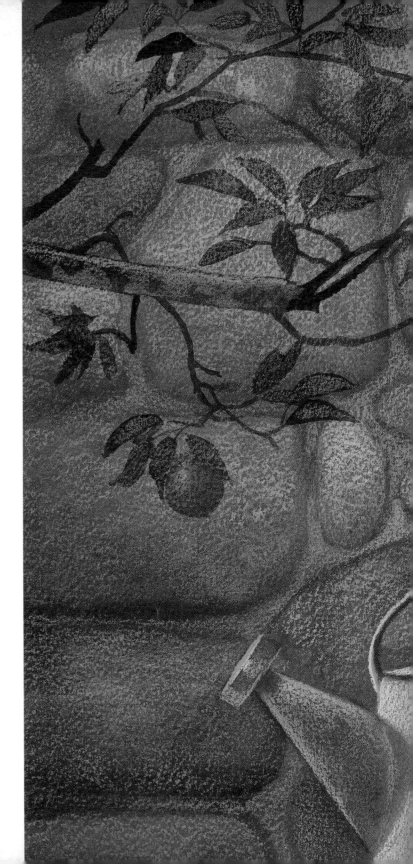

When Mandy was sure the chocolate chips were well mixed in, she walked over to Grandma and touched her on her arm. She pointed to the bowl and Grandma handed her the cookie sheets. Mandy could have used her voice to ask for them—Grandma never winced when Mandy spoke—but she wasn't sure if she would interrupt the sounds of the radio.

She dropped the dough by spoonfuls onto a sheet. It shook as each mound landed. Mandy wondered if cookies made a noise as they dropped onto the metal. She wanted to ask, but Grandma seemed to be dreaming as she rubbed the shiny pin on her collar between her finger and thumb.

When the sheets were lined with cookies, they put them in the oven and Grandma set the timer. Mandy never needed to watch it; she knew the cookies were done when the smell filled the kitchen and went halfway down the hall.

"Mandy," she saw Grandma's lips say. "Grandpa...I...dance...song." She watched Grandma's lips form the words, knowing there were others in between that she didn't understand. Grandma pointed to the radio and pulled Mandy to her feet. She moved the radio to the floor and turned one silver knob. Mandy kicked off her shoes.

Grandma seemed to float as Mandy shuffled across the kitchen floor doing the 1–2–3 dance she had learned when she was little. She knew the name of it because Grandma always repeated the numbers as they danced. Sometimes she could feel the sound of the radio through her feet, and she tried to imagine how the sound might feel in her ears.

Too soon for Mandy, Grandma released her. "Song finished," she signed. It was one of the silly rules of the Hearing World. It would make more sense to stop dancing when you wanted to stop, instead of letting that box decide.

As if she knew what Mandy was thinking, Grandma took her hands and started dancing again. This time Grandma's lips only smiled, and with their eyes they told each other of the fun they were having.

When the smell of the cookies was thick, Mandy stopped and looked in the oven. The mounds were flat and light brown. Grandma handed her a potholder, then turned off the oven and the timer. She poured two glasses of cold milk while Mandy filled a plate with warm chocolate chip cookies. Then she led the way to the living room.

Before she sat down, Grandma took the family photo album out of the cabinet. She pointed to it, raising her eyebrows, and Mandy quickly nodded and signed yes.

Grandma stopped at her favorite picture. Smiling, she pointed to it, then to the pin at her neck. The picture showed Grandma and Grandpa standing under a banner that said 25TH ANNIVERSARY. Grandpa was pinning the silver circle onto Grandma's dress.

Mandy's favorite picture had "*Grandpa and Amanda—age 2½*" written under it. A handsome, solid man stood proudly holding a pigtailed toddler in the crook of his left arm. They were smiling at each other, his head turned just enough for Mandy to see the arch of his hearing aid behind his ear.

Mandy loved her nickname. When people called her Mandy, their lips curled up at the ends almost like a smile. And when Grandpa had said her name, the ends of his mustache had turned up too, making a double smile.

She could have looked at photos all afternoon, but Grandma tapped her on the wrist and pointed outside. "You want...walk?" she asked.

Outside, the light was beginning to soften. Grandma leaned over and wiggled her pin to show Mandy how it sparkled. Then they walked across the yard holding hands.

On the path through the woods, Mandy felt the leaves crackle under her shoes. The branches seemed to wave a friendly hello, and Mandy wondered what they sounded like. Grandma had told Mandy that leaves made small noises when the wind blew them. Since branches were so much bigger, Mandy reasoned, they must make really loud noises.

In a clearing at the top of the hill, Grandma looked up and pointed. Eleven geese flew above them in a lopsided V. Mandy knew geese honked and supposed they sounded much like cars.

The sun was low in the sky, almost in front of them. Mandy stood in a patch of sunlight. It felt warm and strong, and she wondered how it sounded as it passed through the trees. She thought all the noises outdoors must hurt Grandma's ears. That was probably why there were never any people in the woods with them. It was too noisy.

Suddenly Grandma grasped her collar. "My pin!" she said. Mandy could see the panic in Grandma's eyes. She felt her stomach tighten. She couldn't remember ever having seen her grandmother without the pin.

They searched the ground beneath them, first standing, then on their hands and knees, but the pin wasn't there.

Long, limp grass covered the clearing. Scattered stalks of brown weeds stood as tall as Mandy. Her hands grew sore from pushing them aside. Sometimes when the weeds bounced back into her face, she closed her eyes and forgot where she'd been looking.

Grandma walked with her head down, searching near the woods. Mandy went to join her. As they retraced their steps into the woods, Grandma stopped and looked back as if she knew the pin was there and she didn't want to leave it.

They continued looking as they walked slowly along the path. Mandy didn't want to miss an inch of ground, so she kept her eyes down. She looked up only twice, to make sure that Grandma was nearby.

At first they were careful not to disturb the leaves. Then they tried scattering them with their feet. Mandy found a stick so she could move the leaves more carefully; but every time she pushed a leaf aside, she was disappointed. It didn't matter how hard she strained her eyes, she couldn't find the pin.

The sky was bright gray and the shadows had disappeared. Mandy's sneakers glowed against the speckled grass. She shivered. Grandma lightly touched her shoulder. "Come," she said, and motioned toward the house.

Grandma put the roast in the oven and began making muffins. Tears streaked her cheeks. Mandy took the string beans to the sink. She let the cold water run through her fingers as she stared out the window into the darkness.

Mandy hated the dark. It made her so alone. She remembered how frightened she'd been when she went camping last spring with her Brownie troop. At night she couldn't sign to her friends or see anyone's lips. It felt as if the world ended at the edge of her flashlight beam. She startled when people stepped into the light or, worse, tapped her on the shoulder from behind.

Mandy closed her eyes. She imagined her grandmother's bare collar and she remembered how light glinted off silver. Maybe I *can* find it, she thought.

When she opened her eyes, Grandma was not in the kitchen. Mandy slipped her jacket on and grabbed the flashlight from the counter. She carefully closed the door behind her, remembering that Grandma could hear it if she let it shut too quickly.

Flashes of far-away lightning turned the black sky an eerie gray. Sometimes Mandy could see even the twigs of the trees, but they no longer seemed friendly. Her skin was covered with goosebumps.

She took a deep breath and zipped her jacket, then turned on the flashlight and walked toward the woods. Her teeth chattered as she swept the ground with her light. Her jacket kept out the chill from outside—but she shivered as if she had stayed too long in a cold lake.

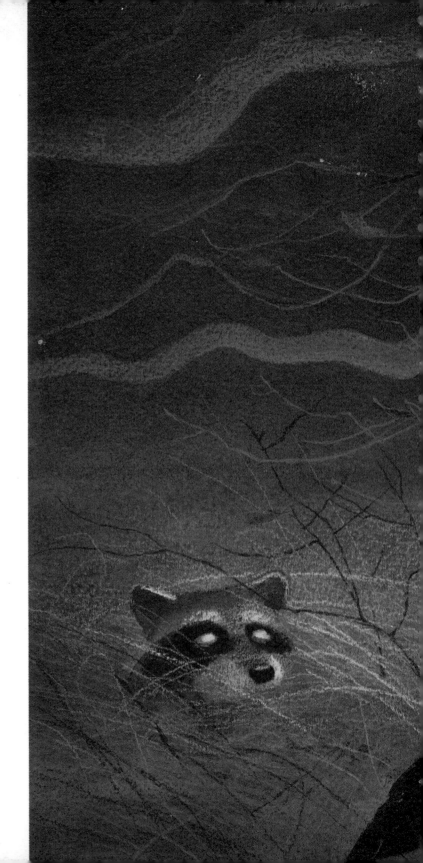

Mandy felt something watching her. She combed the woods with the light, then stopped. Two bright circles of light shone back at her. Mandy froze. "Go away." She felt the words pass between her lips. "Please go away." The eyes disappeared, leaving gray fur and a striped tail in the beam of light.

Mandy held the light on the raccoon until it was far into the woods, then started along the path again. Her heart pounded. At last she reached the clearing.

She took a few steps, then paused and gasped. A wall of black clouds was rolling toward her. Lightning flashed behind them, illuminating their monstrous shapes. Her heart beat so quickly she could hardly breathe.

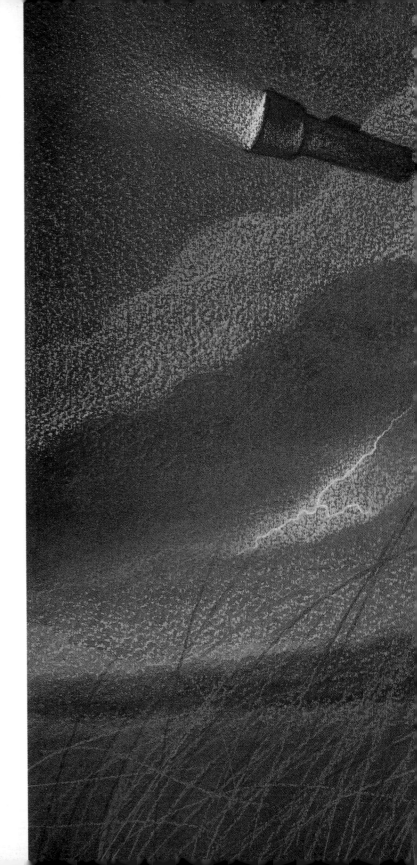

Focusing her attention on the beam of light, Mandy forced herself forward, lifting clumps of grass with the toe of her sneaker as she made her way down the trail she and Grandma had made that afternoon. Gusts of wind whipped the tall weeds into her face. A flash of lightning lit the grass around her. Mandy looked up to see the racing clouds filling the sky. The ground beneath her seemed to shake. She knew she would have to go back soon.

Suddenly she tripped in a small hole and tumbled down. Her flashlight flew into the air and landed a few feet away. I'll never find Grandma's pin, she thought as she lay sprawled on the ground. Another bolt of lightning struck. Mandy caught her breath and rubbed the tears from her eyes. She reached for her flashlight.

Then she saw it. From under the grass came a small twinkle, barely visible in the circle of light. For a moment Mandy didn't move or even breathe. Then she carefully separated the blades of grass with her fingers. It seemed that the pin shone more brightly than it ever had before. She lifted it tenderly out of the grass and pushed it straight down to the bottom of her pocket.

The wind rocked the branches as Mandy ran through the woods, but she kept her light on the path and didn't look into the trees even when the lightning lit them. Her heart still beat quickly, but now it seemed to help her run faster.

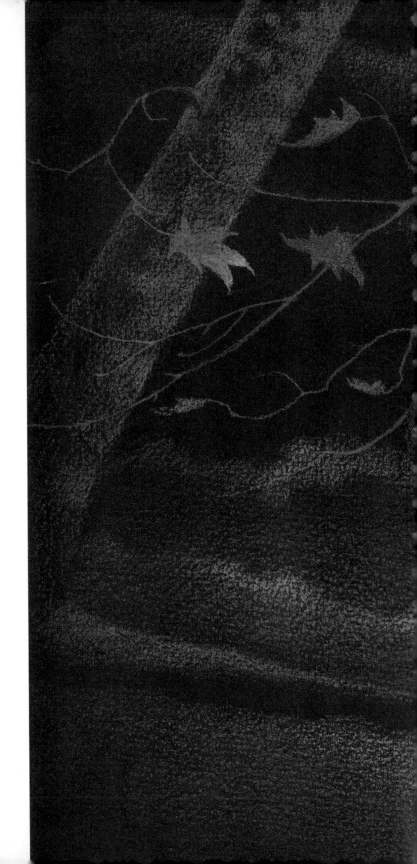

She burst out of the woods, gasping for breath. Grandma ran to meet her. Mandy felt tears drop on her head as they hugged. Grandma's bare arms were cold, and Mandy could feel her hands trembling.

Mandy stepped back. She reached deep into her pocket and pulled out Grandma's pin. It felt cold inside her fist as she held it out. Slowly, she uncurled her fingers.

Grandma's mouth dropped open. Her hands flew to her cheeks. "Oh, my," she said. Her fingers moved down to her lips and she lowered her hand outward in the sign for thank you.

Softly Grandma squeezed Mandy's hand. She took the pin and held it close. Her face was shining. Then arm in arm they walked back to the house as the rain began to fall.